2002 POP MUSIC HITS
Instrumental Solos

ORIGINAL SHEET MUSIC EDITION
ACROSS THE STARS
(Love Theme From *Star Wars*: Episode II)
Music by JOHN WILLIAMS

ORIGINAL SHEET MUSIC EDITION
CELINE DION I'M ALIVE
Recorded by CELINE DION on Epic Records
Words and Music by KRISTIAN LUNDIN and ANDREAS CARLSSON

ORIGINAL SHEET MUSIC EDITION
jim brickman
beautiful (as you)
as recorded by jim brickman featuring all-4-one on windham hill records

ORIGINAL SHEET MUSIC EDITION
SOAK UP THE SUN
Sheryl Crow

ORIGINAL SHEET MUSIC EDITION
The single from her first major motion picture release,
britney spears
crossroads
i'm not a girl, not yet a woman
Recorded by BRITNEY SPEARS on Jive Records

ORIGINAL SHEET MUSIC EDITION
CAN'T FIGHT THE MOONLIGHT
(Theme from COYOTE UGLY)
Words and Music by Diane Warren
COYOTE UGLY

ORIGINAL SHEET MUSIC EDITION
TO WHERE YOU ARE
Recorded by josh Groban on Warner Bros. Records
Words and Music by RICHARD MARX and LINDA THOMPSON

ORIGINAL SHEET MUSIC EDITION
A Thousand Miles
Recorded by Vanessa Carlton on A&M Records
Words and Music by VANESSA CARLTON

Project Manager: Carol Cuellar
Art Design: Olivia D. Novak

contents

A THOUSAND MILES

Words and Music by
VANESSA CARLTON

Chorus:
To Coda
mp
mf
1.
2.
Bridge:
mp
mp
mf

D.S. 𝄋 al Coda
Coda
mp
rit. e dim.

ACROSS THE STARS

(LOVE THEME FROM *STAR WARS*®: EPISODE II)

Music by
JOHN WILLIAMS

Appassionato
f
mf
mp
rit. e dim.

BEAUTIFUL (AS YOU)

Words and Music by
JIM BRICKMAN, JACK DAVID KUGELL
and JAMIE JONES

Slowly and freely (♩ = 66)

Verse:
Chorus:

© 2002 Universal Tunes, A Division of Songs of Universal, Inc., Brickman Songs,
EMI April Music Inc., Doxie Music, Mimi's Music Man Productions and Dayspring Music, Inc.
All Rights for Brickman Songs Controlled and Administered by
Universal Tunes, A Division of Songs of Universal, Inc.
All Rights for Doxie Music Controlled and Administered by EMI April Music Inc.
All Rights for Mimi's Music Man Productions Controlled and Administered by Dayspring Music, Inc.
All Rights Reserved

1.
2.
Chorus:
rit.
freely
a tempo
rit.

CAN'T FIGHT THE MOONLIGHT

Words and Music by
DIANE WARREN

2.
Bridge:
mf
f

ESCAPE

Words and Music by
DAVID SIEGEL, ENRIQUE IGLESIAS,
STEVE MORALES and KARA DIO GUARDI

Moderately fast (♩ = 126)
Verse:

Chorus:

Chorus:

1.
2.

1.
2.

HERO

Words and Music by
CHAD KROEGER

mf
mp
Bridge:
Chorus:
f
rit.
mf

I'M ALIVE

Words and Music by
KRISTIAN LUNDIN and ANDREAS CARLSSON

cresc.
mf
Chorus:
Bridge:
f
Chorus:
rit.

I'M ALREADY THERE

Words and Music by
GARY BAKER, FRANK J. MYERS
and RICHIE McDONALD

Chorus:
To Coda
1.
2.
Bridge:
D.S. al Coda
Coda
rit.

I'M NOT A GIRL, NOT YET A WOMAN

Words and Music by
MAX MARTIN, RAMI,
and DIDO ARMSTRONG

Bridge:
Chorus:
1.
2.

ONLY A WOMAN LIKE YOU

Words and Music by
MAX MARTIN, RAMI,
R.J. LANGE and SHANIA TWAIN

Bridge:
mf
Chorus:
f
freely
mf

ORIGINAL SIN

Music by ELTON JOHN
Words by BERNIE TAUPIN

Chorus:
1.
mf
2.
mf
rit.

SOAK UP THE SUN

Words and Music by
SHERYL CROW and JEFF TROTT

Verses 3 & 4:
To Coda
D.S. al Coda
Coda
rit.

THANK YOU

Words and Music by
DIDO ARMSTRONG
and PAUL HERMAN

Verse 3:
Chorus:

THIS TRAIN DON'T STOP THERE ANYMORE

Words and Music by
ELTON JOHN and BERNIE TAUPIN

Slow swing (♩ = 50)

Verse:

mp

3

𝄋 *Chorus:*

mf

To Coda
1.
2.
mp
Bridge:
f
D.S. al Coda
mf
Coda
3
rit. e dim.
mp

TO WHERE YOU ARE

Words and Music by
RICHARD MARX and
LINDA THOMPSON

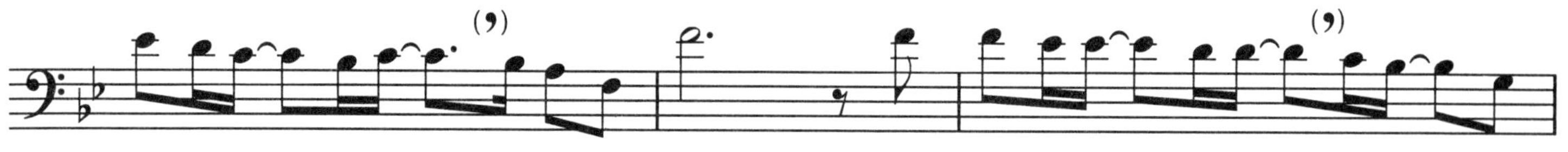

To Coda
Verse:
mp
mf
(,)
D.S. al Coda
rit.
Coda
rit.
mp

YOU

By JIM BRICKMAN,
DANE DE VILLER and SEAN SYED HOSEIN

D.S. 𝄋 al Coda
𝄌 Coda
mf
cresc. poco a poco
Chorus:
f
mf
rit.

I HOPE YOU DANCE

Words and Music by
MARK D. SANDERS and
TIA SILLERS